This book belongs to

_____

Walt Disney ®

RHYMES AND RIDDLES, GAGS AND GIGGLES

WALT DISNEY FUN-TO-LEARN LIBRARY

A BANTAM BOOK

NEW YORK · TORONTO · LONDON · SYDNEY · AUCKLAND

ISBN 0-553-05525-9

Published simultaneously in the United States and Canada. Bantam Books are published by Bantam Books, Inc. Its trademark, consisting of the words "Bantam Books" and the portrayal of a rooster, is Registered in U.S. Patent and Trademark Office and in other countries. Marca Registrada. Bantam Books, Inc., 666 Fifth Avenue, New York, New York 10103. Printed in the United States of America. 19 18 17 16 15 14 13 12 11 10

Classic® binding, R. R. Donnelley & Sons Company. U.S. Patent No. 4,408,780; Patented in Canada 1984; Patents in other countries issued or pending.

Why do bees hum?

Because they don't know the words.

Why do cows wear bells?

Because their horns don't work.

What happens after you are five years old?

You get to be six years old.

What's the difference between an egg and a skunk?

If you don't know, remind me never to send you to buy eggs.

What's the best way to catch a squirrel?

Go up a tree and act like a nut.

What looks most like half a cheese?

The other half.

What must you do before
getting off a bus?

Get on it.

What do you get when you cross a cow and a duck?

Milk and quackers.

What word do you always say wrong?

Wrong.

Which side of a dog has the most hair?

The outside.

Who can jump higher than a skyscraper?

Anyone. A skyscraper can't jump.

What should you do when it's raining cats and dogs?

Be careful not to step in any poodles.

Why did Goofy throw butter out the window?

He wanted to see the butterfly.

What do you have when your head is hot, your feet are cold, and you see spots in front of your eyes?

A polka-dot sock on your head.

What time is it when an elephant sits on a fence?

Time to get a new fence.

If the Three Little Pigs were under one little umbrella, why didn't they get wet?

It wasn't raining.

"Doctor, when my hand gets better, will I be able to play the piano?"

"Of course."

"That's great. I could never play the piano before!"

"Did you know it takes three sheep to make a sweater?"

"I didn't know sheep could knit."

"Did you take a bath today?"
"No. Is one missing?"

Can you see what is wrong with this picture?

"Knock, knock."
"Who's there?"
"Pig."
"Pig who?"
"Pig up your feet or you'll twip."

"Knock, knock."
"Who's there?"
"Duck."
"Duck who?"
"Duck, here comes dessert."

"Knock, knock."
"Who's there?"
"Boo."
"Boo who?"
"Don't cry, little baby."

"Knock, knock."
"Who's there?"
"Candy."
"Candy who?"
"Candy elephant fly or can't he?"

"Knock, knock."
"Who's there?"
"Banana."
"Banana who?"

"Knock, knock."
"Who's there?"
"Banana."
"Banana who?"

"Knock, knock."
"Who's there?"
"Banana."
"Banana who?"

"Knock, knock."
"Who's there?"
"Orange."
"Orange who?"
"Orange you glad I
didn't say banana?"

What if honeybees went to school?
There'd be lots of spelling bees.

What if pebbles could play the trumpet?
They'd have a rock band.

What if front doors could talk?
They would say, "Shut me up!"

What if kittens were tracing paper?
They'd be copycats.

Can you see what is wrong with this picture?

Can you say the word to finish the rhyme?

On Saturday night, we stay up late,
And eat our dinner off a

When you're good, I always bake
A double-layered chocolate

Here is my eye, and here is my nose,
At the end of my feet, you see my

I keep my pretzels in a can,
And I fry my eggs in a

When I go to sleep, I dream
About a bowl of pink

When the day is nice and sunny,
Bears go out and eat some

Leaves are green, and roses are red,
When I'm tired, I go to

If I found a furry fox,
I would keep him in a

Fish gotta swim, birds gotta fly,
I gotta eat blueberry

When a green thing hops upon a log,
I always hope that it's a

The thing that horses do all day
Is stand around and munch on

When I want to travel far,
I do not walk, I take the

Can you say this?

She sells seashells by the seashore.

And this one, too?

Silly Sneezy shears six silly sheep.

How quickly can you say this?

How much wood would a woodchuck
chuck if a woodchuck could chuck wood?

How about this one, too?

Mickey makes a mighty muddle mopping mud.

Can you see what is wrong with this picture?

Find the two words that rhyme to make the answer.

What is an elephant's trunk?
A hose nose.

Where do you find out how to bake a cake?
A cook book.

What do you get when you
stand in honey?
Sweet feet.

Where do mice live?
A mouse house.

What is a kitten caught in the rain?

A wet pet.

What is a silly rabbit?

A funny bunny.

What do you get when you drop your chocolate bar at the beach?

Sandy candy.

What is Donald's pickup called?

A duck truck.